A DUNWICH ODYSSEA

by

Sara Smith

with

Pete Mendes

New Platonist Collective
Publishing

ISBN: 978-1-8381496-3-5
A CIP catalogue record for this book is available from the British Library

1 – Liverpool Street Station

Sara Smith reports from the Observer's new travel series...
With the opening of the new rail line, the Observer has invited us to make the journey as part of its low carbon, car free series.

Restored from the Beeching cuts in a multimillion restoration project, the new line takes what is often called the scenic route, between London and Dunwich; the restored route of the railway line cuts eastward across the country of Essex to the sea before following the coast of East Anglia up to Dunwich. With plenty of sights on route before the destination, our travel team will be travelling slowly to map out a holiday itinerary for the tourist/traveller who wants a low carbon break.

Dunwich itself, as you may have heard, is a location of controversy in these post-fact times. A minority, but a loud one, the Dunwich-deniers, claim that the ancient university city is an elaborate hoax, and that the famed city is merely in reality a few cottages and a shingle beach. The mainstream opinion is of course that the city - whilst fairly inaccessible and impervious to regular photographic techniques - is well documented and definitely a real and fun place to go to on holiday. Fear not reader, into this morass of swirling myth and claims of imagination and truth we will bravely step and report first-hand on the true state of affairs.

We gathered at Liverpool Street Station where the train was to depart.

In our party, myself to give a report; Mendes who is our restaurant and accommodation reviewer; Lara the photographer; and Julia. A bit about each of them, as they will be integral to our trip.

After the unfortunate fallout from the last series of articles I covered, the Observer has sent along Julia from Finance who had the company credit card. I have worked with Lara on our previous report on the Voyage of the neoTitanic (now ex-neoTitanic as the prefixes mount up). As a joke she has brought along for me *A Brief Guide to Impulse Control* - not that anything was ever proven - which I may read if time allows. Mendes is already stuck in a corner, feet curled up underneath, reading something by James Joyce. I don't think he wants to come on this road-trip rail trip.

The train itself, it seems, is seeking to cash in on the continued popularity of the Harry Potter franchise and waits gleaming and puffing at the platform. Decked out in vintage wooden compartments and an atmospheric dining car, it transports us back to the golden age of the railways. I feel a thrill of excitement as the train begins to move, taking out my trusty pencil, Ms Sharp, from my inside pocket, starting to pen this account of our journey. This, truly, is the way to travel.

From Pete Mendes:
Perhaps it is unwise to expect too much from a railway dining car, given the limited cooking facilities on board, and so upon entry I ensured that my hopes were suitably muted. However even the abysmal standards which I had pessimistically foretold were thoroughly disappointed by the **Dunwich Express Area for Dining**. This dining carriage aims to be reminiscent of what they call the golden age of train travel but is MDF with a cheap veneer. It boasts of organic seasonal produce cooked in a rustic Italian fusion style. Which would be fine, only it is mainly reheated from plastic containers. As it was breakfast time I ordered the poached egg panini, which turned out to be something tasteless and rubbery in a flaccid white oval. As for the tea, I have never before experienced microwaved tea. Now I know why.

2 - Pernall Templars

Pernall is the village idyll that we have been waiting for: thatched houses, village green, old church, wood beamed pub, riverside walks. All half an hour from London, for a countryside fix against the grime and crime of our great capital.

If this were not attractive enough Pernall also houses the historic King Arthur Appreciation Society (KAAS). Based in the Arthurian Temple - a sandstone octagon upon a low-lying hill just outside the village - KAAS is the leading group which keeps Arthur's memory - or legend - alive, organising historic reconstructions, banquets and readings from Mallory.

We are met by Mystreal at the station, the representative from KAAS.
'Hi I am Mystreal.'
'Is that you real name?' I asked.
'What is real?' she replied enigmatically.
'I mean, is that the name that HMRC uses for your taxes?'
She didn't reply, but led us to the temple.

Atop the green hill we passed through the doorway into the shadowed interior. Here stood an assembly of motley armoured knights and variously medievally bedecked folks mixed with those in more modern attire. The single room rose into a dome above us, with several layers of platforms skirting the walls, forming a sort of viewing gallery.

For a better view we were taken to a platform overlooking the octagonal inner chamber. 'And here is our key artifact,' explained Mystreal.

What looked like a jewelled window allowed mottled light to seep into the crypt like atmosphere, and it was this window display that our attention was directed upon.

Incorporated into a stained glass reredo was the grail itself, a dun cup, with various elaborate twirls.

'This is the famed Grail,' explained Mystreal. 'It has various mystical properties and is literally at the centre of all we do here, our great quest and aim.'

'Do you mind if I have a closer look?' I asked.

'You must not touch it!' she said sharply. 'It is a venerable historical artifact and can only be handled carefully by trained professionals.'

'Not even a little stroke?'

'It is prophesied that grave consequences will occur if an unbeliever's hands should grasp our great treasure.'

'Prophecy, smophecy.'

'In any case, turn around and look below, for we have arranged a display of feats of courage for you today.'

Unlike other organisations which have to rely upon the dark arts of politics and slippery compromise, the Knights are able to offer an altogether cleaner form of conflict resolution. They put on their armour and fight.

'It is no longer to the death,' explains Mystreal, 'we do have some concessions to the modern world.'

We are in for a treat today because a duel has been scheduled to resolve a key ideological dispute.

The Quixotians believe that Arthur was a real knight and King and that he is (still) calling others to be knights and to live out a life of chivalry. These people reject the trappings of the modern world and travel around on horseback, having adventures. In contrast, the Analogists consider Arthur to be a legend, an expression of the eternal Knighthood which all are to nurture in their hearts, whilst living lives in all other ways identical to others in the modern world. To some extent both groups had managed to coexist, but after several months debating whether to remove the requirement for armour wearing, the disagreement became so acrimonious that there was only one way to resolve it: a fight.

From the Quixotians, Sir Edrick Dragontooth; from the Analogists, Mr John Jones. After the archaic preliminaries steel clashed with steel and the clanging and scraping of a sword fight began. However it was more boring than I expected, with both combatants being rather geriatric, and mainly consisted of sharp lunches forward separated by long periods of intense and malevolent gazing.

Tiring of the repetitive nature of this violent pecking, I turned to the grail. Considering that it was a famed and legendary item I thought that they might at least give it a good polish now and then. Peering into its depths I began to make out characters in a curled script, chiseled into the metal. With an accelerating pulse I wiped with my sleeve the area, for perhaps now I would uncover a discovery that would change everything. The light being poor in the temple I still could not see the lettering clearly. I thought I would quickly lift it to see before returning it at lightning speed.

It was a little stiff so I applied some force.

It seemed as if the grail had been incorporated into the structure of the temple, as its capstone, as its central and ordering brick, that on which all else depended and rested. And so when it was removed...

Cracks spread outward from the gap, radiating rapidly throughout the stones of the building. There was a rumble from above, from below and the floor beneath us was tossed to and fro. A violent shaking seized us and we could hear the grind of stone upon stone and the ggrraah of tearing timber. All upon the platform were thrown outward as the wall became rent asunder.

We fell backwards, rolling down the green hill as the great temple imploded behind us, crushing all inside it, utterly destroyed.

The cup still in my hand, I could now see the lettering clearly. It said:
M.K. Haussweissen, Club Darts Champion 1934

From Mendes
If you like tacky cash-ins with sub-standard offerings, Pernall is the place to come. We dined in the **Camelot** which dubs itself a gastropub and is thoroughly decorated with knights, grails, magicians and enchanted swords. The menu items are from the Brakes Wholesalers ready meal catalog, passed on for ten times the price. Night brought us **Round Table Hotel**, which featured many ridiculously loud squeaking floorboards all through the night, which rendered sleep impossible. I can only presume that some of the residents were playing a fast-forwarded version of Sir Gawain. I wish I could pull a Garwain on the proprietors of the hotel, dishing out to them a torn-up back from the hard bed.

As for the destruction of the ancient knight-temple, I blame Sara.

3 - Mersea Mythological Zoo

It is something of an advantage to the relaunched zoo on
Mersea Island that the new train line passes opposite its
entrance. More by accident than design the zoo now has access
to a steady stream of visitors from afar. This is no longer a
provincial anomaly and curiosity, but a star attraction.

The owner, eccentric millionaire Bertie Raffles, appears visibly
excited as we meet him outside the entrance. Springing with
energy he leads us through the turnstiles into the zoo.
'It was an inspiration,' he tells us. 'To bring all these creatures
under one roof. It has become an obsession of mine these past
ten years.'
'But are they some sort of model, these mythical creatures?'
'They're quite real,' he said.

Out of the entrance we find ourselves in a courtyard filled with
the most beautiful statues of people beholding mythical beasts.
'Another hobby of mine,' Bertie adds, 'I'm quite the collector.'
'They are fascinating,' I say. 'Incredible workmanship.' The party
trickles through the statues, examining them, anticipating the
creatures they will soon see, before Bertie herds us towards an
arched passageway.
'We do have an array of regular animals, but I'm guessing you
are here to see our mythological section,' Bertie says, and before
we have the chance to ask another question our first sight greets
us.

We pass through the regular animals with barely a glance, barely
registering even the ferocious looking lions. Moving swiftly
through iron gates into the mythological section, we see signs
pointing to enclosures; the flaming plumes of a phoenix; the
spurt of a fiddywinkle; the beautiful winged horses; the fierce
minotaur. But we were rushed past all these trails that we might
see the prime exhibit first. As we walked I questioned Bertie:

'How do you come to acquire these creatures?'
'It is hard for me to say without breaking certain confidences,'
he replies. 'But at the very least I can say this: if you have enough
money the word 'impossible' does not exist. There are certain
contacts in Siberia…'

'Now,' says Bertie, 'I do ask you to be careful with our next
creature. As with all our creatures we have taken adequate safety
precautions. However, a special warning is required. Make sure
that you only look at this creature through the mirror. It is of the
utmost importance. Do not look at the creature directly.' Once
we had assured him that this is what we would do, we were let
into the tassel-doored underground lair.

'There is a name which chills the heart and tenses the gut:
Medusa. A woman with snakes for hair and whose direct gaze
will turn a person into stone.'
'Um er excuse me I am sorry to interrupt your er reverie but
Gorgon is the name of the species. Medusa was only a specific
Gorgon.'

Fortunately she was locked away in a secure room and the only
way of seeing her was through a one sided mirror that was in
effect a giant periscope.

But when it was my turn, try as I might, I could not see
anything. Perhaps it was the dim light of the room or the
ephemeral nature of the beast itself but I couldn't make it out. I
strained against the mirror trying to see something, anything.

It is hard to say exactly how it happened.

I was leaning against the mirror, eager and searching, when there
was a cracking sound which seemed to emanate from me. It was
my beloved pencil, Ms Sharp, snapped in two. I didn't notice at
first, consumed with mourning for my pencil, but it appears that

the slumped impact of that very sharp lead caused a perforation in the mirrored surface which spread outward. Soon the mirror was collapsing upon itself. The cry went out to beware. But it was too late for Lara. The Gorgon had fixed her with its stare and she had been turned to stone.

Once the Gorgon was made safe by attendants and we had recovered from the shock, Bertie started to manage the practicalities, firing questions at us.
'Does Lara have a family - perhaps they would like her statue in their garden - or else we could keep her here in our foyer?'
'I don't know.'
'She has a parrot,' said Mendes.
'Would her parrot like-'
'I don't think the parrot cares one way or the other,' said Mendes. 'Would you like us to ask it?'
'Yes that would be excellent. We just have some paperwork to complete...most unfortunate...'

From Mendes:
Unusually for a zoo, the **Mersea Zoo Cafe** offers the opportunity to dine upon its residents, as a form of population control. It is rare as a restaurant critic to find something genuinely new, but here I can honestly say that I have. All is freshly prepared on this limited menu, based on what creature has been slaughtered; on the daily menu today was grilled koala with parsley butter (delicate with a hint of citrus) and griffin steak (richly marbled with a sweet and nutty taste) with a wild garlic jus. All with an Olympus of freshly baked bread, newly churned butter from Apollo's cows and oranges for dessert. As for drinks, I recommend the Ambrosia.

At the **Zoo Hotel** there are a range of sleeping arrangements possible, even including the chance of spending the night in the lion's enclosure. After asking why it wasn't dangerous, I was

handed a 500 page liability release contract which I would have
to sign should I elect to stay with the lions. Apparently it is
popular with divorcing couples, bachelor parties and men named
Daniel.

As for the events which ensued in the zoo, I blame Sara.

4 - St. Osyth Lifeboat Club

The brief journey on the train from Mersea elapsed in silence, Mendes reading something by Sebald, and Julia looking out of the window, whether with sadness or fear I find it hard to say.

But onwards, to St. Osyth Lifeboat Club. Whilst there is currently a legal dispute over SOLC's claim to be the oldest lifeboat organisation in Europe, there is no doubt that it has a great deal of tradition behind it with the only extant Tudor boathouse. It has a pill-box green lifeboat, an effective education and outreach programme, an extensive bar with over two hundred different varieties of malt whiskey, a dramatics society - the Old Raconteurs, and remains still the only boathouse with a professional level theatre. Add to this the corporate hospitality suite, money raised for charity by its energetic committee, its heritage work and of course the Michelin starred restaurant, and the SOLC is a hive of activity. But we visit it in troubled times. An acrimonious argument is storming over aspects of the governance of the Lifeboat Club. Chairman Henry Broughton explains to me beside the gleaming green lifeboat.
'The established trustees on the board, such as myself, are fighting a rear-guard campaign against our recently, regrettably, appointed Centre Manager. It is a battle for our very soul.'
'What ever is the matter?'
'The Manager, a pugnacious man named Ivor, is a devotee of a narrow philosophy which is something of a poison amongst the old lifeboating societies. We have seen many boathouses succumb to these new trends of thought. But we are determined that we will not fall.'
'So he doesn't respect what exactly?'
'He advocates throwing away the traditions which have built up over time. The traditions that link us to our fathers. All that we have worked so hard to construct and preserve, and to think how much my grandfather contributed to this Society, it is like

Ivor is spitting on his grave. Never mind, we will manage to oust
him soon.'
'Can you be any more specific about what exactly has happened.'
'He wants to take away our lifeboat from us.'
'That is terrible,' I say.
'Yes it is, isn't it,' says Henry, touching the boat fondly with a
hand. 'Here it is sitting, only yesterday some school children
came to admire it.'
'What on earth does he want to do with it?'
'Why, sail it, of all the preposterous things.'
'Sorry?'
'Yes, that's right, you heard right, though I'm not surprised
you're stumped for words by the heinousness of the action. He
aims to take the lifeboat out from the boathouse where it is
perfectly preserved and positioned for our educational and
corporate activities. And put it out on the open sea.'
'I am not an expert in these things,' I said. 'But I assumed that
was the point of a lifeboat.'
'I can see their propaganda has reached you,' said Henry darkly.
'As you can see we have a wide range of activities here at St.
Osyth. We have a richness to our activities that bring wide
ranging benefits. When people like Ivor come along and
effectively suggest shutting down all our wonderful activities to
just concentrate upon this one single idea of jaunting around on
the sea, well, it is narrow, it is impoverishing, it is dehumanising.'
'And the lifesaving at sea?'
'There is more than one way to save a life,' said Henry. 'I could
tell you stories of isolated pensioners given a new lease of life
through our dramatics society, the children in Africa saved from
starvation by our fundraising activities, and - speaking for myself
- being launched into the fullness of life by our wide selection of
fine whiskeys.'
'I have to admit, I'd never thought of it that way before.'
'Yes indeed,' said Henry. 'And most important of all to oppose
the distasteful philosophy behind this narrowness of thought.
How monstrous to suggest that people are perishing in the sea. I

don't want to believe such dreadful poppycock. How awful, and how judgemental, to believe there are those plunging and floating, shouting and shrieking, cursing and struggling and drowning in the dark angry waters. People in the sea don't need to be rescued. They are perfectly fine as they are.'
'Yes it is a very stark picture of life and death this Ivor seems to have.'
'Yes, all black and white when in reality there are many shades of grey. But Ivor does not recognise this. However even though Ivor has succeeded in diverting funds to make this exhibit seaworthy again, and although he cancelled our club night to go off so-called life saving on the sea, we are very close to terminating his employment, which will be a great relief.'

I was very impressed with the wide-ranging activities of the boathouse, but with the lifeboat now able to sail once more, Henry and some crew members were able to take us out on a ride.

Bouncing over the waves in the lifeboat was exhilarating. It was a large craft and the waters were our playground. The early autumn winds chilled us as my hair was whipped around me.

When it was almost time to return Henry gallantly offered to give me a turn steering.
'Now,' I said. 'Isn't it on boats that its counter intuitive, that you have to steer the opposite direction than you think.'
'No, just steer the way you want to go.'
'Are you sure about that because when I was five I had this toy boat.'

The boat covered the ground a lot faster than I anticipated. Its turning curve was also more limited than I imagined. So when the shore approached at increasing speed I pulled as hard as I could.
'No the other way,' Henry shouted.

'Oh dear Thor no,' I cried out.
'Stop stop!' shouted Mendes.
'It won't just stop!' I said.
'My boathouse!' Henry shouted like a dying man.

CRASH!

We emerged unhurt. The same cannot be said of the boathouse which was smashed into smithereens.

From Mendes:
We were due to dine in the **Lifeboat Dining Room**. However, that was before Sara drove the lifeboat into the clubhouse. Nevertheless, there is a crab stall which we were able to buy some lunch.

We travelled on, spending the night in Harwich.

5 - Harwich Joy Centre

To cross the river Orwell at Harwich a giant bridge has been
built across the estuary. It soars upwards, somewhat
unnecessarily, in a hyperbola, the tallest structure for miles. Not
to waste the sightlines that this produces a viewing platform has
been constructed at the centre. And on this platform is Harwich
Joy Centre.
'Just don't make the bridge fall down,' said Mendes, as the train
rose up.

The view, both out to sea and inland, is impressive on the
platform, but it is the Joy Centre itself which truly amazes.
'Imagine the feeling of the purest ecstasy,' said inventor and
entrepreneur Rudolf Hamm.
'Thinking of my rampant rabbit right now,' I said.
'That,' he spat Germanically. 'You insult me with the lowness of
your expectation.'
'What then?'
'Imagine a call, a song, so compulsive that you couldn't say no to
it.'
'I've never done crack but I would be open to it. For journalistic
purposes obviously.'
'No, it is more of a longing than an addiction. Maybe I am
explaining it wrong.
We are all incomplete in ourselves. We are driven to gain certain
goods. Some of these good things are very practical and
complete, but the more interior they get, the more abstract and
transcendent. So for instance we desire sex and the release of
drugs and alcohol. But we also desire friendship and love. And
belonging and security and worth and adventure and freedom
and connection. And so on. Well imagine that you managed to
cut right into the heart of a human and find the most intrinsic
and basic and deep desire of all. I don't have a name for it which
will do it justice: but I do have the solution: my Harwich Joy

Centre. The more technical name is what you might call a Reality Adjustment Device.'

'How does it work?' I asked.
'Very simple,' he said. 'A pod is released from this platform, fully equipped with our advanced technology, and before the pod gently hits the water below, joy is achieved. It is powered by the newly discovered Octavin particle.'
'I have never heard of Octavin.'
'You wouldn't have unless you were a particle physicist.'
'What are we waiting for then? Let's try it. Let's get to J.O.Y.'
'A word of warning. There is one possible side effect from experiencing this joy. A side effect not entirely proven, but which I must make you aware of. For legal reasons.'
'What is it?'
'Death.'
'What?'
'Probable death.'
'Death?'
'The process of the release of Octavin - according to some of our models - vaporises the human subject. And to some extent that is backed up by our experimentation: when we go to check the pod the traveller is most often absent, presumed vaporised. My own explanation is that the person inside is transported to a new plane of existence.'
'So, you can have an experience of the pinnacle of human existence but it will kill you.'
'Indirectly.'
'Many takers?'
'Quite a few in January we find.'

The three of us were shown around the pod. It was fairly small, only large enough to seat one person, and all white, except for the shiny black screens.

'Very impressive,' I said at the end of the tour. 'But I don't think
that we will be trying this out, unlike our other trips where we
get involved.'
'Very well,' he said. 'Not thrill seekers then?'
'Ha! I don't want to speak for myself! But Mendes only really
cares for books and food and Julia, well, Julia is an accountant.'
'Let us move on then to the-'
'I'm not a square you know,' a voice said quietly. It was Julia.
'I know.'
'I can have fun. I can be wild.'
'I am sure you can.'
'I once travelled at 32mph in a 30 zone. It's not just you
journalists who do crazy stuff.'
'Yes well done.'
'Blast it. I'm going to go in the pod.'

'No its not worth it. Please Julia,' Mendes said. 'Tell her.'

I tried.

Julia got in the pod. She was sealed in. The siren called out. We
watched as the pod was released. It descended to the water
below, landing softly in the Orwell Estuary and floating.

At the bottom we looked into the pod. She was gone.
'She has ascended to a new existence,' said Rudolf.

The accounts department will send a new credit card person
called Graham.

From Mendes:
Yes the Joy Centre has a cafe. No I don't feel like reviewing it.
Am I concerned I will make it out of this trip alive? I am sure
that Sara will have as much success with us as Odysseus had
with his crew members on his journey.

6 - St. Felix Howe

Descending the bridge by train we travel to St. Felix Howe.

'Why couldn't you just leave her alone?' Mendes said on the
train.
'I didn't do anything.'

Nestled between the Orwell estuary and the sea is a promontory,
on which stands a green hill, topped with a low grey tomb.
Around the base of the hill, a small town gathers. This is St.
Felix Howe, our next stop.

Bede describes St. Felix landing as a missionary in East Anglia
on the back of a dolphin and then exploding across the eastern
counties in a wave of conversions and piety. Quite how much of
Bede to take at face value is uncertain, but there is certainly
some grain of truth. If Dunwich was the city that Felix ruled
then St. Felix Howe is his burial place.

We walked to the top of the hill on arrival. It was windy and
there wasn't really anything to do so we turned tail to explore the
town.

The Howe (as the town is known locally) boasts a fine fish and
wine market and the settlement is very much a home for the
adjourd oui.

Mendes shows me the fish market.
'Most British people will only ever eat a few different varieties of
seafood. Cod. Salmon. Tuna. Prawns. Seabass if they think
they're gastronomically refined. But there are-'
'Plenty more fish in the sea,' I completed. There they were, all
laid before us in crystalline ice, a shockwave of saltwater and
iodine which assaulted our noses. Cetasta. Ugly brutes.

Turbot and monkfish and fishese. Sturgeon. Urchins. Many
more that I could not recognise.

Mendes was in his natural environment, chatting with the
fisherfolk about their offerings. There was a fair amount if
glugging in evidence also.

Looking up some notes while eyeballing a particularly large
monkfish, I remembered that it was here also that acclaimed
director Natasha Lybrihov has a residence, and it just so
happens that I spied her in the corner of the market, in a cafe.
She was cracking open giant Selkie eggs and eating the innards
raw with buttered toast, all washed down with expensive looking
champagne. We were poured a glass each.
Hey hey, I said. 'Natasha.'
'Hello and who are you.'
'Sara I am with the Observer.'
'Take a seat,' she said.

Natasha, of course, is the illustrious director of acclaimed
television show HoshiHenro. It was to the show that I directed
my line of questioning.
'One season left to go, what do you have planned for the final
part of Hoshi-Henro?'
'You will remember the end of season 5?'
'Yes absolutely. The fleet is confronted with the spacewhale and
they have to decide what to do. Will they kill it? Or follow it into
the unknown. Killing it will give enough Octavin for a hundred
years of life in space. But could it lead us home?'
'Quite.'
'So which do they choose?'
'I won't spoil the ending.'
'Maybe you could do multiple endings!'
'Fun, but rather lazy narratively. Have some conviction about
your own story, I say.'

'But you could leave it to the viewer to decide, it is more
democratic.'
'It is possible.'
'Big question though: which ending would be real?'
'You tell me.'
'But only one thing can actually happen. Either something is real
or it is not.'
'Has it ever occurred to you that we ourselves might be part of a
fictionalised serialisation? That we who think we are real are
merely constructs of another time and place…'
'No I never thought that.'
'Exactly.'

We continued drinking expensive champagne and were soon
joined by Mendes. A cultural snob, he refuses to admit to
watching television, and so affected disinterest in Natasha; yet a
hypnotic interest in overpriced food and drink kept him
anchored to us.

At some point Natasha must have left though I can't remember
when because it had turned from morning to night somehow.
It's still all a bit mixed up in my mind. We might have drunk a
lotWe stood on the prom overlooking the waves, trailing bottles
in our hands.
'Drink,' he slurred.'Drink, sweet oblivion, come unto me.'
'Here you go.'
'You know,' he said. 'You are leaving a trail of death and
destruction behind you as we travel.'
'Accidents do happen!'
'It is the grotesque tale of disaster.'
'You have to laugh or cry I suppose.'
'And death, hoary death.'
'I prefer to laugh myself.'
'Though many poets have spoken of our secret longing for
death, for utter blissful annihilation, leaving the self behind.'
'Do you want a fruit pastille?'

'And the little death.'

Then he kissed me, for some time, before slinking away.

From Mendes:
What can I say? I am repulsed by myself, that in weakness I snogged her. Thank goodness it went no further. In my defence: she was wearing a shoulderless dress. Her shoulders are very alluring. I disgust myself.

7 - a field

We continued on the train, just the two of us. Mendes tried to read *Akenfield* whilst I tried to engage him in conversation.

'Look Sara,' he said. 'You know from the beginning that you should have done this properly and written your account in poetry. After all, you are putting a Homeric spin on it by the title. If you can't manage iambic pentameter then at least try blank verse.'

Mendes spoke a mighty force
Assailing hearts and so resolve rose
To meet the challenge and forsooth
Fortunately after primary school poems don't have to rhyme.
Or scan.

The train slowed in yellowed field
With no station to show in our sight
Why we were stopped in empty land
When we were not scheduled to.

And, hark! quoth I, for before the nose
Of our mechanical behemoth train
A kerfuffle erupted.
Turning seeking espying
Mendes sought the source of such eruption
Turning sharply
Books spilled out of his bag
Shelley and Joyce and Homer
All mixed and jumbled.

And forsooth
I gazed forth through the window
Surely there is a more poetical word for window
Portal maybe or limpid portal.

Anyway.
There a sight which shook my soul.

Blood - vermillion or was it carnelian -
Sprinkled splattered spotted,
From my nose
Sprung out aghast at what i saw.

A girl, a handmaid, no more,
Stood before the beachéd bulk
Lone figure small and sad and solemn
against the armoured shell

Her eye was bright, her lance was keen
Clothed in spacesuit girdled round
Her courage etched in every seam
On the track her feet stood firm
Defiant and strong and -

Behind her a looming shape
That I didn't see at first
A sodding spaceship.

Sleek and shining stood its loins
Strong its armour
Indomitable its force
Fast its engines with ligh'ning thrust.
With pointed prow and noble mast
It lay there on the bank.

Do you see this I quoth to Mendes.
See what he replied.
The spaceship you bellend.

There's just a couple of bikes, said he.
So I jumped off to speak to the girl

at the centre of it all.

O gentle maid said i.
Why jump before this metalled beast?
Are you desirous for it to
Maul your limpid form?

To slay quoth she, blushing deep
For this spacewhale must be vanquished.
Spacewhale? Asked I.
Cetastra, she clarified.
Sorry, still no, I said perplexed.
Have you ever seen series 4 of the scifi tv show hoshihenro? She
said.

From Mendes:
She should stick to prose. Just because she is writing poetry,
there is no need for this faux epic style.

8 - Orford

The train stops in the shadow of the ruins of Orford Castle, a
broken down ruinous type keep from I don't know the
Normans or one of the Henries or something. I'll try to find out
before publication.

On the journey the skies have been looking glum and as we
arrive gobs of rain start to decorate the windows.

In a caf with steamed windows and rain clattering like pebbles
we peered out at the ruined castle in one direction and the
wrathful sea in the other, a clutched tea warming our dampened
clothes. It was here that we met Dr Howard Leigh, gospels
expert, to fill us in on the mysterious Orford Gospels.
'Many have heard of the Lindisfarne Gospels,' he explained. 'But
the Orford Gospels remain more obscure.'
'Why is that?'
'I imagine that it is the scrotal illuminations,' he said.
'Oh, I thought that they were mysterious creatures of legend and
folklore.'
'No. Research has decisively proved that these markings are, in
fact, all variations of a ballsack.'
'Fascinating. Can you tell me the significance of these gospels?'
'Yes they are noteworthy for containing material considered
alternative gospel accounts, containing as fragments of an
ancient and marginalised tradition.'
'So a sort of rival to the mainstream gospel accounts.'
'Indeed and they are very old.'
'So, can we see them?'
'Yes absolutely.'
'Lead the way!'
'Oh you mean now and here. They are held by the British
Library in their Yorkshire collection and several weeks notice are
required. You can see them, but not in Orford and certainly not
today.'

We were cowering under our umbrellas to inspect the ruins when in the rain soaked soddy gloom Leigh took it upon himself to explain the fine background of Dunwich:

The city of Dunwich, capital of East Anglia, was famously saved from the encroaching waves through the ingenuity of the ancient coastal defences before the great 1286 storm; a large chunk of the town of Aldeburgh to the south had fallen into the sea. The old city was shaped by its ten historic colleges. The four along the seafront; Greyfriars, Barts, St. Leonard College, St. Martin College; with their own private beaches. The two big colleges at the centre of town around the marketplace; St. John's College, St. Peter's College; the chapel of St. Peter was known as the cathedral of the marshes and resembles a ship sailing out. The two oldest and most prestigious colleges were located in the south-east of the city, Blackfriars and Temple College. St. Francis sat to the north, its long lawns leading to the River Dunwich. The Victorian All Saints in the east completed the list of colleges in the old city.

Dunwich Institute of Education, which gathered up the singular colleges into one organisation in the 1880s, had only recently rebranded as Dunwich University; many of the old signs with the previous acronym were retained by stubborn academics or inconvenient architecture. Which was very confusing for new students confronted with what seemed an implacable instruction in the lobby of the physics building in ten foot high concrete built into a supporting wall.

Whilst tracing its history back to the middle ages, it was in the 1940s that its most distinctive element was introduced to the university. The Institute had won the bid for the Atomic Research Science Experiment; the UK's nuclear research project. Construction was quickly completed on the High Energy Physics Building – a great white gleaming geometric dome

beside the sea - and experimentation on a range of theories had
begun, working in cooperation with the Manhattan Project in
the USA. It was the research into electromagnetic pulses that the
scientists in HEP B advanced most impressively, becoming
world-wide experts. These pulses however had a drastic effect
upon the city of Dunwich. Whenever an experiment occurred,
and the pulse went out, all electronic equipment that was not
protected by a wire cage was damaged, often beyond repair.

Bereft of electricity, Dunwich became a city marooned in the
past, an island linked to civilisation (if Saxmundham can be
called civilisation) via steam train. No cars (spark plugs), no
refrigerators, no computers or internet or telephones, no electric
lighting, no radios or recorded music, no McDonalds. It became
an idyll for luddites, anacrophiliacs, warm beer enthusiasts, and
escapees from the patterns of modern life. And the tourists.
Trainfuls of tourists. A slice of olde Englande served up, a must
visit in all the guidebooks, a city wide theme park of Austen and
Dickens and Sherlock Holmes. Buoyed by the large university
and a never-ending rotation of tourists, the city was able to
afford the streetlighters, washerwomen, milkmaids, porters and
stables that such an anachronistic situation demanded.

My college, Cecil Rhodes College, was created in the great
expansion of the Institute in the 1960s. Work at HEP B was
suspended for a year to allow for the building of new
department buildings and ten new colleges, and the new campus
was based to the north of the river Dunwich. The resulting
panorama of concrete and glass contrasted against the medieval
streets to the south, and those submerged in nostalgia for an
imagined past – incarnate in Dunwich city – were aghast,
vilifying the Institute and and Council for allowing such
monstrosities. By the present day several of the buildings had
been recognised as architectural gems of the 60s and were now
Grade 1 listed. The brutalist Guthrum College, formed of great
long slabs of concrete, designed by architect, Le Corbusier, was

chief among these. Wuffingas College, a miniature of the
Alexandra Road Estate, built by Neave Brown was not far
behind. Fawcett College, with its womblike structure designed
by Oscinda Lucido, was unique. Even Oliver Cromwell College,
comprised of a fifty foot photorealistic erect phallus, was at least
something to talk about. Cecil Rhodes College was not one of
these noteworthy buildings. It was a squat structure with a
peaked roof, and could have functioned equally as a school,
prison, hospital or retirement home.

From Mendes:
It was at this point that I walked away. For your sanity I have
requested that the account be cut off here. I am not even sure if
all Leigh said was strictly speaking, true. It also seemed as if he
thought he was flirting with Sara.

9 - Sunken Aldeburgh

Aldeburgh is one of those sad places which used to exist.

Local historian Peter Armitage joins us as we walk along the
gravelly shore.
'It was a series of coastal disasters in the middle ages which did
the damage. Before that Aldeburgh was a thriving seaside port
and centre of the fishing industry. But several storms reduced
this from a great city to a town. Until recently there was some
dwelling here, a couple of churches standing. But one by one
they have fallen to the waves. There are only a few buildings left
now, and in time they too will be eaten up.'
'Some pin the blame on the city of Dunwich, or so I have heard,'
I said.
'That is a very popular theory, that the changes made to the
Dunwich defences in the 1200s led to sand being deposited at
Dunwich which would otherwise be here, that same sand
protected Dunwich from the storms whilst leaving Aldeburgh
vulnerable. But there is no way of going back and testing the
hypothesis. There is another thesis regarding the river Alde but
again, nothing can be proven.'
'Fascinating. There are a lot of theories.'
'Yes, and none more fantastic than the novel *Quintet* by Amelie
Roane which is set in a fictionalised and reimagined Aldeburgh.
In this alternate timeline it was Dunwich that was washed away
by the waves. Aldeburgh remains a charming coastal town, and
the place where the plot plays out.'

Despite the absence of any town, there is no empty expanse but
a range of activities: Aldeburgh Amber Hunters, a Relationship
Counselling Retreat Centre and a few snack huts. We had
secured an appointment at the Relationship Centre. The retreat
centre is based in the airy art deco Marnet Masion, and run by
Helen Igbertsson, the Swedish lifestyle guru. The retreat centre
has been in the news, recently welcoming a string of celebrity

couples, and has won an award for the daring construction of a tidal swimming pool built on top of the ruins of Aldeburgh.

'Welcome, welcome,' says Helen in the immaculate lobby. 'Let me show you around, and introduce you to our therapeutic philosophy. Intrinsic to our couples therapy is our tidal pool.'
'How is that?'
'In the high tide of love there are many sunken dangers beneath the surface, but it doesn't really matter, because you float far above them. They seem irrelevant to you. But a time comes when the tide ebbs away and the water becomes more shallow. Now as you swim you collide with the submerged debris, which you still cannot fully see but which scrapes and crashes against you.'
'What sunken protuberances might a couple find?'
'There are many possibilities, but most often we find that it is the submerged power dynamics of a relationship. You see, every human relationship comes with a power dynamic: at any one time the amount of power is going to be unbalanced. One person is going to have more control than the other. It is natural, and in many cases power fluctuates freely as the stages of life pass. But in many other cases, the power structure has become fossilised into a master-slave relationship.'
'Sounds a bit BDSM.'
'I am not talking about sexual dominance, what is in view is the flows of mastery and submission: who is trapped and who is free.'
'And you therapy involves getting people back to high tide?'
'Not exactly, no. Because high tide isn't necessarily any better than low tide. In some ways it is worse, because you are labouring under the delusion that there are no flesh-splitting dangers beneath you. At low tide you are in many ways more true to yourself.'
'So what do you do here?'
'We get a couple to swim in the pool at high tide; and then repeat the exercise at low tide. Then, after bandaging their

wounds, we get them to name the submerged elements in their relationship.'

The tidal pool itself was large and wave washed.
'You have a go, no?'
'We're not a couple,' said Mendes.
'We did kiss,' I reminded him.
'But that was-'
'I am sensing a relationship out of kilter,' said Helen. 'Whatever the nature of your relationship we can do some work on it here. We also do corporate team building days after all, for those in the workplace.'
'Of course you do,' said Mendes.

We lined up beside the pool, shivering in our swimming gear. Turns out Mendes in tiny tight speedos is hot. Pity Lara is no more or I would have got her to sneak me a pic for personal use.
'Doesn't it matter that it's low tide?' he said.
'Not really,' our Scandinavian guide said with perfect indolence.

The water was very cold, North Sea cold. We were gasping. I might have squeaked. We started to swim the prearranged number of lengths, and soon we began to kick against items submerged below the waterline. Still, we seemed to be managing well with the challenge. Until after three lengths I got cramp and Mendes had to carry me back. It was heartwarming and relationship building as he lifted me safely onto the ice-fingered concrete. However as I crawled up an involuntary spasm twitched my thigh. Mendes was pushed backwards through the air, landing awkwardly. Fortunately, Helen and her team were able to fish him out before he drowned, and all that he suffered was a broken leg.

Helen was delighted by the progress we had made in our relationship.

From Mendes:
Inevitably the retreat centre itself will be destroyed by coastal erosion at some point in the next ten years. Good riddance.

10 - Dunwich

It has been a long and eventful journey, and yet as we near our destination my excitement mounted. Dunwich is unique in the modern world. A place of wonder and history and whimsey.

The train turned the final corner, out of a brace of trees. I looked for the city. But it was not there. Where were the spires and bell towers? Where were the ancient colleges and hallowed lawns and learned stones? Where was Dunwich?

A blasted heath, a darkling plain. A wretched bog leading to the sea; its waters drawn off by the vanishing tide, subdued and distant. I listened, and heard only the grating roar of pebbles which the waves drew back and flung. Until this too drew into silence.

The station was little more than a stab of concrete, surrounded by marsh. Standing, apparently waiting, with a walking stick, was a wheezing old man, more of a ghoul than a person.
'So you've come heehaw,' he said to me.
'I think there must be some mistake,' I said. 'This must be an extra stop before the final destination.'
'Nope, this is Dunwich. Look, end of the track there.'
'Then, what? Is this some kind of joke?'
'You were a believer, were you?' said this man.
'The city of Dunwich doesn't require belief. It's existence is a fact. It is in history books, geography books. I've read about what has happened here in newspapers. There are even dim photos of the place. There are institutions based here.'
'Heehaw?'
'what?'
'Everyone believes in something. How do you even know what your eyes see is the world as it is? You don't know, you have to believe.'
'But that's nonsense.'

'Your face is nonsense, stupidface. Heehaw.'
'There's no need for that.'

We both stood, listening and looking. I rubbed my eyes and blinked, just in case. But nothing changed.

'So Dunwich doesn't exist. Not like I thought.'
'Either that or your eyes are broken.'

Looking out to the nearby sea, I only hear its melancholy, long, withdrawing roar, retreating, to the breath of the wind, down the vast edges drear and naked shingles of the world. What is this, some sort of mind-mess play by Samuel Beckett?

From Mendes:
It is fair to say that I have been a sceptic of this journey. I never wanted to come on this fake road trip on a train. But as the train turned the corner and Dunwich came into view, I repented of my former dismissiveness.

A forest of spires puncture the clouded heavens, sunbeams pouring down through the holes, ladders to glory. The salt air suffuses the town, pocking its ancient sandstone with spat cherrystone indentations. Narrow lanes of cobbles overhung with medieval beams lead into public squares full of statues and traders with hot floury potatoes and the smell of sausages cooking. Huge vaults of subterranean libraries with lost islands of ancient manuscripts spread underneath, dotting the streets with air vents and curious trap-doors. The garishly modern colleges to the north of the town, the 1960s campus, with its individual and baffling ornaments collected together into one mass. Quiet lawns and cloisters full of shrieking students. The endless shush of the waves and the intermittent roar of the train. The old lighthouse pumping out hot light through the hours of darkness. The sound of cows being milked in the early morning.

Places to stay and eat are plentiful and there are many gems to be found. I am not entirely sure what happened to Sara, but I stayed at the Saxony Hotel, opposite St. Peter's College in the Market Square. Considering the constraints it was a very comfortable stay, though there was simply not enough hot water.

Of the restaurants, notable is the **Tern Bakery**, producing the iconic Dunwich bun, a whisky infused marmalade pastry, sticky and sweet and bitter. The perfect breakfast with a cup of their freshly roasted Golem Brew coffee. For lunch, take a trip out on one of the small fishing boats near the harbour to catch seafood: on return the fisherman will fry it up on a Bunsen stove in a ramshackle shed with lots of butter and a bit of lemon and stuff it in a white bap.
Eat when it's so hot it burns your mouth, with mug of tea, leaning against the splintery panels of the shed, whilst regaled by dubious ocean stories and indecipherable sea shanties. For dinner my top pick is the **Carnivale Fantastique**, which occupies a tall and narrow tower in the south of the city. First established in the 1830s it currently offers a menu focused upon - bizarrely - smoked ribs, doughnuts and cocktails. But it all works and is calculated to perfection. And, in addition, the waiting staff is formed entirely of trained pixies.